Rock Art *Romance*

A Southwestern Novelette

Also by Kayla Oliver

Blossoms of My Desert Home
A Collection of Photography, Art, & Poetry

Light and Love
A Collection of Christmas Poetry

Rock Art *Romance*

A Southwestern Novelette

Kayla Oliver

the bohemian life

To my soulmate Donovan.
Thank you for your everlasting love and support.

&

To my dogs, past and present.
I love you all dearly and
you are *always* in my heart.

Chapter 1

The citrine sun rose over a distant plateau, sparkling in the September sky and illuminated the sprawling desert landscape as my Jeep sped along the lonely old highway. Joshua trees cast long shadows across the sandy red dirt dotted with sagebrush. Roadrunners raced across the two-lane road while falcons perched on powerline posts, eyes darting and alert for breakfast.

I relished it all. The Southwest and all its splendor. Tires humming and radio playing, composed the sound of adventures to come.

With my best friend Chase by my side, today was off to a great start. Chase is my hiking and adventure buddy. He's chunky and lovable, always up for a fun hike, and he gives lots of slobbery kisses . . . Yeah, my best friend's a dog. An adorable golden retriever.

Windows rolled down, breathing in that fresh desert air, I smiled at Chase who had his nose out the window and wagged his tail. He was always as excited—okay maybe even *more* excited—than me for a day of hiking.

I turned up the volume on the radio as "Return of the Grievous Angel" began to play. I sang along with

Emmylou and harmonized with Gram.

Classic song. It was one of my grandpa's favorites. I let out a bittersweet sigh as fond memories of him flooded my mind. My grandpa was my biggest teacher in life. He taught me so much.

My lips rose into a half smile as I recalled how he used to tell me legends and stories. A particular favorite of mine was "The Legend of the White Doe." It was about the importance of deer and their symbolic nature.

He'd start out by asking, "Now Callie, did I ever tell you about 'The Legend of the White Doe' my granddad used to tell me when I was just your age?"

I'd giggle and pretend I hadn't, even though he'd told me at least a dozen times before. I decided from a young age that you've got to humor elderly folks, especially ones who love storytelling as much as he did. And besides, I always did love hearing him tell stories.

"The legend says that deer are spirit messengers," he'd begin, his face becoming serious, but with that ever-present twinkle in his eye. "Deer, particularly a white doe, are a sacred symbol, a messenger of good fortune to come."

I would look up at my grandpa, mesmerized and eager to hear more. I'd ask, "What kind of good fortune?"

"Well, it could be riches, adventure, a good crop, love, or simply an opportunity for your soul to grow. No one can predict it for certain. We cannot know what is written in the stars for us. Everyone's path in life is different. Remember that."

Being the romantic I am, I secretly hoped my great

opportunity of good fortune in life would be for love. A great love like in the storybooks my mom would read me at bedtime. A hero and a princess. Two souls meant to be together, who overcome evil, and *always* live happily ever after.

"The legend goes like this," he'd start the story. "Long ago, a young woman whose parents had been killed in a raid, went into the forest to gather berries with woven baskets in hand. Her bare feet silently tread across the forest floor. The morning sun shimmered through the trees and gently illuminated the berry bushes ahead of her. She spent hours picking berries for her tribe's feast and festivities that evening.

"While she worked, she spoke to the Great Spirits, asking for guidance in her life. She was lonely. Lonely for love. Most of her cousins and sisters were already spoken for, with babies of their own. She missed her parents. Her kindhearted mother and her noble father. She wiped away her tears and began walking back to her village with full baskets and a heavy heart. When suddenly a white doe ran across her path, the sun shining a spotlight on her before disappearing among the dense forest trees. She gaped at the beauty she witnessed and sent a silent offer of gratitude to the Great Spirits for sending her that sacred symbol of hope. That evening at the festivities, she met and fell in love with a handsome fellow who was visiting from a neighboring village."

My little heart full, I would sigh contentedly and beg to hear the story again. I once asked my grandpa if *he* had ever seen a white doe. He told me he had. He'd caught a glimpse of one as a young man, and the very next day he met my grandmother, the love of his life.

My grandpa was the reason I chose the career I did. From a young age he instilled in me a love of the outdoors and local history. Growing up I wore out countless pairs of hiking boots, trekking along with him on adventures and spent many winter evenings warming up by the fireside while listening to his tales of local history, legends, and lore.

Working for an organization dedicated to the research and protection of public lands and their historic sites as a historian and assistant archaeologist was a dream come true for me. I was on my way to a little known rock art site where I planned to photograph and research the petroglyphs, check the site for signs of vandalism, and jot down notes and any additional research needed for an upcoming article I'd be writing.

The farther I drove away from the city, the lighter my soul felt. I smiled to myself as I imaged each mile marker cheering me on, "Yeah Callie! Wahoo! You go girl!" Getting outdoors often, and on a Tuesday, was definitely a perk of my job.

I pulled off the highway to top up on gas at a small mom and pop service station. The old building was complete with tumbleweeds and faded signs. Rustically beautiful. The morning was already heating up, so I zipped off my jacket, balled it up haphazardly, and threw it in the backseat next to my gear. While Chase relieved himself and the gas pumped, I stretched, yawned, and double checked the map.

I put Chase back in the Jeep and he reluctantly settled in his seat. After a pat on the head and saying I'd be right back, I ran inside the gas station for some snacks. The bell on the door jingled as it opened and without missing a beat the cashier called, "Beautiful mornin' ain't it."

"It sure is," I replied cheerfully while striding to the refrigerated section to grab a bottle of orange juice. I had overslept, *thanks Netflix*, and didn't have time to grab breakfast as I rushed out my apartment door that morning. My stomach was starting to protest.

Heading toward the counter, I picked up trail mix, grabbed a bag of Jolly Ranchers and plopped them down for checkout. Greeting me with copious amounts of blue eyeshadow and a crispy hairspray framed face was a smiling cashier. *Marge,* according to her name tag.

"Would ya like a blueberry muffin to go with that orange juice, honey? My sister-in-law baked 'em fresh this mornin' and thems are the best darn muffins I ever had."

"Count me in, that sounds delicious!" I said with real enthusiasm. My mouth watered at the heavenly aroma as Marge grabbed a muffin from the cloth lined wicker basket and put it in a brown paper bag. She folded the top over and handed it to me while I slid her a twenty. I put the change in the soda cup labeled "tips" mostly because my hands were full.

"Why thank ya sweetie! Drive safe now ya hear?"

Marge called out after me.

"Will do, you're welcome," I replied over my shoulder with a slight wave and a polite smile as I exited the store.

I tossed my newly acquired "breakfast" through the window onto my seat while I checked the tire pressure, cleaned off the windshield, and queued up my playlist. Good music is a non-negotiable road trip essential. I was now ready to continue my journey.

After pulling back onto the highway, my stomach could wait no longer and I yanked out the giant blueberry muffin, crinkled the bag, and tossed it onto the backseat. One bite in, and oh boy it did not disappoint! A perfect ratio of blueberries per bite. I made a mental note to get another one, or two . . . okay make that three, *don't judge me*, on the drive back home. This was indeed the most delicious blueberry muffin I'd ever tasted.

Kudos Marge's sister-in-law.

Chapter 2

Time passed smoothly along that straight desert highway. Roads like these are relaxing, pristine views and the steady rhythm of my Jeep roaring down the road. *Sixty-five stay alive.*

After another forty-five minutes on the road, I approached the dirt road turn off. Using my blinker and slowing down, a gigantic silver Dodge truck sped by, blaring his horn the whole way. "Yeesh!" I muttered under my breath. Apparently he couldn't be bothered to wait for half a second. I slowly shook my head, "Some people."

The dirt road was in decent shape, slight washboards, but not too bad. The scent of sagebrush and dust filled the car. I quickly rolled up the windows, much to the dismay of Chase, who smeared nose marks on his window in protest.

I scarcely enjoyed the scenery because there would be two additional turnoffs to keep my eye out for. I had been to this rock art site once before, but it was years ago with my grandpa, and we were having so much fun that I was oblivious to the route we took. Besides, what young kid *actually* pays attention to routes and directions?

I missed driving down dirt roads in my grandpa's old truck. It was entertaining, adventurous, and serene, all wrapped up into a, "half-ton chunk of metal, fueled by diesel," experience. Old songs played on the radio, my grandpa's baritone voice belting along. He'd tell jokes and stories as we traveled together through God's country. They were good times . . . the best times of my life.

After a fun day of exploring, a young me would usually fall asleep on the way back home, serenaded by the hum of the highway and my grandpa singing. I'd snuggle up in the old Mexican blanket he always kept in the truck. Worn out, but extremely happy.

At the end of every hike, my grandpa would get into his truck and blow the accumulated dust in his nose into his ever-present red bandana. After folding his handkerchief, he never failed to say, "Callie, you know, people say they pick their nose, but I feel like I was just born with mine."

Now remembering his jokes made me want to chuckle and cry all at the same time. My heart ached from missing my grandpa. Seeking comfort, I reached over and stroked Chase's furry back.

I pulled to the side of the road to wipe a few errant tears and decided to check the map again. A cloud of dust engulfed the Jeep as a truck with a white horse trailer passed by.

Three more miles until my next turn. There should be a marker for it, but I set the odometer just in case.

The second turnoff led to a drastic change in road condition. I adeptly avoided obstacles, deep ruts, potholes, rocks, and mud puddles, thankful for my Jeep and its four-wheel drive.

Not thinking it could get much worse, I soon realized my mistake as I turned left onto the third road that would lead to the trailhead. A glorified ATV trail. *This should be interesting*.

After we crept along, arms tense, and my back singing praises for great suspension and shocks, we finally made it to the trailhead. Chase seemed relieved for the bumpy and winding drive to end as well.

A small dirt parking lot with a pit toilet greeted us. There was a single picnic bench that had seen better days, a faded and torn trail map posted on a weathered wood stand, and a small plaque indicating that this was the project of some long-ago Eagle Scout. Surprisingly, a Prius was parked there, complete with the obligatory political bumper sticker. I was impressed their car was able to make it.

Swinging my legs out of the Jeep, I slipped off my suede moccasins, pulled on teal wool socks, and laced up my well-loved hiking boots. I stepped out into the mid-morning air and stretched my shoulders to relieve the tension from driving.

I placed a few snacks in my pant pockets. Easy access snacks *are* important. I twisted up my dark brown hair into a high bun, applied lip balm with SPF, and popped a watermelon Jolly Rancher into my mouth. Chase sniffed around the trailhead and enthusiastically marked his territory on the fence post.

After getting my gear sorted, I shrugged my backpack

onto my shoulders, tightened the straps, and took an exhilarating deep breath. I was excited to stretch my legs and let the day's adventure begin.

Chapter 3

Even toward summer's end, the days in the desert can still get scorching, so I was glad I opted for a white tank top. I swung open the top gate while Chase eagerly leapt over the rail onto the sandy trail. I couldn't help but smile as the gate closed behind me.

The first few steps of a hike always boost my mood and I had to keep reminding my legs to pace themselves and not get carried away excitedly skipping. Chase on the other hand *couldn't* reign in his excitement and dashed ahead.

As usual, for the first mile or two, he would run back and forth. Charging up the trail, then loping back to trot by my side, smiling at me the way dogs do. Then his excitement would get the better of him and he'd sprint ahead again. Eventually though, if the hike was long enough, he would realize he'd need to conserve his energy and be content hiking by me the rest of the way.

The narrow red dirt trail wove through striking desert flora. I stopped several times to smell the creosote bushes and observe the various vegetation. I admired the yellow desert marigolds and the globemallow with coral pink blossoms. The late summer rains had made the desert come to life with beautiful blooms. After only a few hundred yards I *had* to stop again to take a quick picture of a cholla cactus framed in with cinder knolls and red cliffs behind it. *Gosh I love my job.*

I am ever in awe of this diverse desert landscape. A cloudless blue sky blissfully contrasted the blazing sun. "The bluest skies on Earth," my grandpa would say. Sunshine warmly caressed my shoulders as we hiked on.

Along the way several lizards skittered across our path, and a cottontail darted from sagebrush to sagebrush that scattered across the landscape. I sighed with relief that Chase hadn't seen it. Even as a young pup, it became apparent that he loved to chase anything and everything. Hence his name. He'd *chase* everything.

Butterflies, bicycles . . . his own tail.

Everything.

The trail gradually increased in elevation. A lone juniper tree sprinkled here and there turned into clumps of junipers. Like Bob Ross would say, "Everyone needs a friend."

Continuing on, the sandy pink path gave way to dusty brown dirt. Piles of pellet sized deer scat lay sporadically beneath the juniper trees. After spotting animal tracks, I stopped to take a closer look. Feline! I snapped a quick picture to show my brother later. He's always been interested in wildlife. With signs of a big cat in the area, I would need to be wary.

I reached for my water bottle tucked into the side pocket of my backpack. Chase lapped up the water I poured for him. Splashing water onto my hands, I wiped at the sweat beading on my forehead and neck. I was refreshed and ready to keep hiking at our steady rhythm . . . and to put some distance between us and the cat tracks.

The beauty and solitude was a balm for my soul. The dry desert air that filled our lungs was heavenly. As we hiked, I casually ate trail mix, or "M&M's with obstacles" as my brother likes to call it.

I passed a middle-aged couple with hiking poles and fanny packs. "Obviously the Prius people," I chuckled quietly to myself. I could have pegged them anywhere. We exchanged the necessary "hellos" and the head nod accompanied by the small lifting of the hand that doesn't quite constitute as a full wave.

A few paces passed each other and they stopped and called to me. I was worried they had heard my muttered comment about them being "Prius people" but relief washed over me when they just asked if I was local. They had been to visit the arch and were curious about other good hikes in the area and wanted a local's opinion. After giving them directions to both a slot canyon and an Old West ghost town, they thanked me and we parted ways.

A mile later Chase and I took the right fork in the trail, the lesser used one. Though the term "trail" is a bit generous for it. It's essentially an unmarked game trail. It was never developed like the other trail systems that lead to an arch. This was designed to protect the petroglyph site. You can only get to it if you know where you're going. Okay, hypothetically speaking, *maybe* you'd find it if you wandered off trail a bunch, got lost, and magically stumbled across its location . . . but probably not.

We came to a small stream with big trees lining its banks. I skillfully stepped from one grey stone to another while Chase happily splashed straight through it. On the other side I bent over to pinch off a small piece of watercress. As I raised that green goodness to my lips, Chase shook vigorously, pelting me with cold droplets of water and drool that launched straight into my open mouth! I spat, wiped my mouth with the back of my hand, and sarcastically murmured, "Thank you Chase."

Shadows cast by juniper and pine trees shaded portions of the trail, a welcome relief from the heat of the day. Pine needles cushioned the high desert floor, and rabbitbrush burst with lovely yellow blooms.

The dirt trail inclined, giving way to a steep cinder covered path. I was extra careful about my footing so I wouldn't slip. Loose cinder rock can be like walking on marbles.

After a few minutes I paused to catch my breath and give my burning legs a momentary reprieve. I decided it'd be a good time to check my notebook for the vaguely written directions of what landmarks to look for since I'd soon be off the path and hiking towards the scarcely known petroglyph site. *We should be getting close.*

Chapter 4

I walked by a few pinyon pines dispersed among the juniper and sage. Chase stopped to relieve himself while I paused to check if it was a pine nut year. *Unfortunately it wasn't.*

While avoiding cactus sprawled in clumps, we accidentally spooked two chipmunks who scurried away. Chase inevitably took off after them. I called him back, bribing him with a treat. *Works every time.* "Whoever said bribery was wrong, probably wasn't getting satisfactory results," I said with a triumphant smile.

After climbing an even steeper incline, my legs burned, and I was huffing and puffing for air. We were finally almost to the petroglyphs. The sun was high in the sky, brilliant and blistering in all its glory.

Eventually the ground leveled out as we approached the rock art site. With a sigh of relief and excitement we collapsed under the shade of an enormous juniper tree.

Once my breathing was steady I set up a base camp. A place where Chase could eat and relax while I worked. It's how I keep him at a respectful distance to the delicate pictographs and petroglyphs.

Chase was eager for me to retrieve his plastic baggie

full of kibble. I wiggled out of my backpack, set it gently down on the dirt and leaned it against a grey stone. After digging through my backpack to get his food, I dumped it into a small plastic container moonlighting as a dog bowl. I got out another container for his water and began to fill it. Chase started lapping up the waterfall I poured before it hit the dish. Big droplets splashed off his face and onto the dirt below. After he got his fill, I took a big gulp of water myself, poured some into my cupped hand and splashed it on my sunkissed face. "Hydration can be so refreshing," I giggled to myself. Chase tilted his head in agreement.

Nestled into an alcove at the base of bold red cliffs, lay a dozen black basalt boulders etched with petroglyphs. The canyon opened to a meadow that stretched from the center then climbed to the left, transforming into rolling hills that rose steeper into mountains beyond that.

The west side of the rock art site faced gradient drop offs. Three feet of flat ground stood between the western petroglyphs and the naturally occurring Inca-like terraces. The large boulders dropped off somewhat sheerly in five to fifteen foot increments until it reached the valley below.

I gave a quick look over of the site and refamiliarized myself with the layout of all the panels since I hadn't been here in years. Everything appeared to be in good order. I walked back to base camp for a well-deserved lunch break and to strategize my research and documentation methods.

I sat next to Chase who had already polished off his food, zipped open my backpack and pulled out my sack lunch. A peanut butter and honey sandwich, a nice juicy orange, fruit leather, and a sports drink.

After making quick work of my lunch, my stomach was contentedly full. I felt I had a pretty good idea of how to research the site, so we sat for fifteen minutes simply enjoying the tranquility of the canyon. Crows soared above; their wings silently glided on unseen air currents. Distant birdsong echoed off the sandstone cliffs and the gentle babble of the stream below combined to soothe me with serenity.

I stood and stretched my quads, Chase jumped up to, so I reached into my backpack and gave him a treat. After telling him to stay, he spun around in a circle three times and laid back down with a funny groan. Chase was zonked out before I had my bag back on. I was rejuvenated and excited to get to work.

Starting with the boulders farthest up the canyon, I worked from left to right, and then down. My documentation and research began by taking photographs of each panel in their entirety, then photos of individual glyphs.

The largest boulder's east side panel was massive *and* impressive. I recalled this one in particular from my childhood. I remembered the scene so vividly. Two large bighorn sheep were located in the center of the panel, surrounded by several shaman, a dozen life-size bear claws, and a Kokopelli in the upper left corner. There were different grid patterns too, ranging from simple to intricate. Random small mammals were scattered across the panel. The entire scene was a grand work of art.

I had asked my grandpa what the story meant, but he didn't know the interpretation. I've spent years researching rock art and sometimes there are still things that mystify me.

Climbing over rocks and rustling through sagebrush brought me to the next boulder. The Hunting Panel. This one featured arrowheads, warriors, big game, and Atlatls—which is a type of spear. A straightforward scene of rock art.

The last boulder to photograph was a panel facing west. There were about twenty deer of varying sizes, all facing the same way, though there was one exception . . . One small doe amid larger bucks and fawns that faced the opposite direction. *Interesting*.

I returned my DSLR camera back into its case, put it back in the front pocket of my pack, and took out my notebook and pencil. In my field log I penciled out rough sketches and noted the position of certain glyphs in relation to the others. I inspected if the glyphs were made by pecking, grinding, or a combination of both. I checked for any overlap in the designs and used a compass to determine the precise direction in which each panel faced.

While checking for vandalism, I glanced around the boulder over at Chase, relieved to find him still asleep and hadn't mischievously snuck off. Thankfully there were no signs of vandalism. Vandalized rock art disgusts me.

When I was checking on a petroglyph site only twenty

minutes from my apartment, I was sickened to find it spray painted. At another site someone had tried, and failed, to cut a Kokopelli petroglyph off the panel in hopes of selling it on the black market.

As I worked, I inspected each panel to see if the amount of desert varnish was consistent or varied. Desert varnish happens in dry climates, when certain minerals and microscopic bacteria cling to the rock, gradually building and darkening over time. It's one of the ways we are able to differentiate the age of petroglyphs. If in the same area there are glyphs much darker, almost indiscernible because their shade is nearly that of the rock, then we know they are much older compared to the newer glyphs that contrast brilliantly with the surrounding rock.

I checked for signs of a Sky Watcher—one whose job was to monitor the movements of the sun and the stars, phases of the moon, and the planets in the heavens—to see if it was a potential archeoastronomy site. These sites were designed to coincide with Solstice and Equinox events where light and shadow interact with precise petroglyphs or pictographs. Near a panel with ceremonial figures, I found a marking that indicated a shaman's seat. This was a place where the chief or shaman could sit and watch the archeoastronomy scene play out. Fascinating!

I stopped in front of a small rock and looked down at its flat top where there were three petroglyphs. I couldn't help but smile at the depiction of a dragonfly, a child's right handprint, and an adorable little hummingbird.

Spirals, sheep, and handprints were strewn across several smaller rocks, half hidden by brush and various desert flora. There were also numerous rain clouds and corn stalks depicted.

The archeologist I assist believes this clan had a semi-permanent residence along the riverbank about thirty miles as the crow flies from this site. Though the evidence we've collected has been compelling, we have yet to locate any definitive remains of this theoretical ancient farming village. We did GPR—ground penetrating radar—scans last month, but haven't got any promising leads, *yet*. Last year we found a thousand-year-old seed jar still filled with corn kernels. The pottery was painted with a complex geometric design. It was an incredible find. We've also found archaic turquoise beads and several obsidian arrowheads. All of which now reside in a local museum.

I wondered what significance this location had to the people. Did they have a permanent settlement nearby? Or did they only use this canyon as a camp during the summer months?

Pondering these things, I stopped to sip more water, my face was flushed under the midday sun. I was shocked out of my reverie as I heard frenzied barking. I called out for Chase just as a huge animal sprung down off the boulder! With a flash of fur, it landed right in front of me! I instinctively jumped back, eyes squinting shut, and threw my arms up to protect my throat from the predator. The water bottle flew out of my hand, I could hear it emptying out onto the parched dirt.

When moments passed and my flesh hadn't been shredded to pieces, I peered out from behind my defensive arms, more out of curiosity than bravery. Before me stood a large animal lingering within arm's reach. I gasped and took a step backwards.

Had I seen what I thought I just saw?! A *white* doe! I couldn't believe my eyes! I gasped in wonder. Her coat was angelic white and luminescent. She was the loveliest thing I had ever seen. As she glided passed me, the world slowed. Her warm brown eyes met mine and I felt a connection between our souls. She was beautiful! I was utterly in awe at such a miraculous sighting.

Spellbound, I gazed at the white doe in amazement as she gracefully pranced across the trail, bounded down the rocky terrain, and vanished through the juniper trees. She disappeared just as quickly as she had arrived. Bewildered, I blinked hard and whirled around to stare in the direction she had gone.

As I turned, my feet slipped out from under me on the loose cinder rock, arms flailing, and with a squeal, I tumbled backwards . . .

Chapter 5

Falling over a steep boulder, gathering cuts and scrapes along the way, I strained my neck forward desperately trying to prevent my skull from smashing into the rock. My shoulder blades burst with pain as they struck against the boulder. My hands clutched for anything to cling to. My fingernails dug and scraped against the rock. Efforts to stop from falling were in vain.

Plummeting inevitably down, a piercing shriek rang in my ears. There was nothing to grab on to. The world was spinning and everything was a blur.

I couldn't slow down.

I couldn't stop.

My body lost contact with the boulder and for a terrifying moment I was airborne. Gravity pulled me fluidly through the thin desert air, relentless in its duty. I flipped right side up momentarily, then dropped onto solid ground. The momentum pushed me back. I rolled onto my right ankle awkwardly and fell flat on my back with a thud. My neck whipped back and a plume of dirt puffed out as my head hit the ground. The breath was knocked right out of me.

Disoriented, I gasped in vain to get air in my lungs.

Panicked tears stung my eyes as thoughts of suffocation pounded my mind. Then finally the relief of oxygen filled me and I panted for more. Each breath was a relief accompanied by a sharp and burning pain. The smell of blood made my stomach churn.

I laid in the dirt for several minutes while tears trickled down the sides of my face and pooled into my ears. The saltiness stung my scraped skin. All I could manage was to focus on my breathing. Inhale. Exhale. One breath after another. Pain shot through me and I didn't dare move. I've learned in life that sometimes all you can do in the moment is to *just breathe*.

Eventually, mustering every ounce of strength and courage, I carefully propped myself up onto my elbows, wincing with pain as I eased into a sitting position. I gave myself a quick look over, assessing the damage. I gagged at the sticky trails of blood seeping down my bare arms. Taking a deep breath and focusing on the boulder in front of me, I delicately tried to stand. When the weight of my body pressed onto my right ankle, I cried out in pain and fell back onto my butt.

Closing my eyes, I struggled to calm my ragged breath. Taking hold of the pain, I tried to clear my mind and focus on the situation. Stoicism was what would save me.

I craned my head to take in the surroundings. Below me was an even bigger drop off, and I was walled in by other boulders.

My best chance to get out, was to go up. I needed to get back to where I had fallen from . . . to the top of an eight-foot boulder.

It seemed impossible.

But clearly just sitting here wasn't going to get me out of this situation. With resolve I gingerly rose, trying to avoid putting even an ounce of pressure on my right leg. I limped to the boulder that loomed above me, taunting me with its size. I reached up to feel for a hand hold. *Nothing.*

I leaned my hand against the rock and hopped around to its side, looking for any feasible route. Hope swelled in me as I saw that this side might actually be climbable. I reached far up the boulder, clinging desperately to a small nook, jumped off my left foot, and tried to pull myself up.

While straining my arms, I brought my left foot up onto the boulder, it slipped and the strength in my arms gave out. I frantically swung my right foot up, but the moment it made contact with the rock, pain shot through me, weakening my focus to climb. There was nothing but pain. I dropped down, defeated.

I tried several more times to climb out but to no avail. Drenched in sweat, and huffing from exertion, I turned around to grab my bag for a drink. With a groan I realized that my backpack was still where I left it, by the petroglyphs under a tree.

My phone was in my backpack too and *not* in my pocket. "I wouldn't have had cell service anyway." I sighed, trying to make myself feel a little better. "And who would I even call?" I definitely wasn't going to tell my parents about this incident, since they already don't like me hiking alone. Apparently to them Chase doesn't count as dependable company. In my current predicament I started to doubt my own decisions, but I didn't want to give my parents the satisfaction.

I sat for a while in hopes that my ankle might have a speedy recovery or that I'd miraculously develop enough upper body strength to climb out. I wished some hikers would come this way. As time passed and nothing magical happened, I grumbled, "And I thought white does were supposed to bring good luck. Thanks for nothing!"

I was ecstatic and relieved when Chase *finally* came and peered over the ledge. I tried desperately to get him to fetch my backpack. My mouth was dry. Swallowing had become difficult. A drink of water had never been so appealing in my life. Chase stared at me curiously, whined, then abandoned me to nap in the shade. *A nap, not a bad idea.*

The midday sun beat relentlessly down on me. I undid my bun and let my hair fall around my bare shoulders, hoping to shield my skin from the sun. I was exhausted. The pain emanating from my ankle was excruciating. I leaned back against my nemesis, the boulder, and tried to wipe away thoughts of dehydration. Rest would be good. Then maybe my dizziness would ease and I could think more clearly to devise a plan.

My head drooped and my sandpaper eyes closed. Defeat washed over me. I was ready to surrender to the exhaustion and helplessness of my situation.

And then all went black.

Deep in the sweet serenity of sleep, the throbbing pain began to ease. As I drifted farther into unconsciousness, my current reality became a distant memory. I was no longer stranded in the desert, injured and alone.

I was a kid again . . . eating ice cream at my grandparents' house after a fun afternoon spent running through the sprinklers. The dream was so vivid I felt the velvety ice cream melting on my tongue, its delectable taste filled my senses.

I wanted to stay in this dream and be with my grandpa longer, but was startled awake as "Stay Alive" played in my mind, as if someone were next to me singing the words.

"Open your eyes Callie!" I whisper yelled to myself and gave a slight slap to my face. My voice was hoarse and my throat dry and achy. I murmured, "Open your eyes. I'm not giving up that easily. Stay awake, stay alive."

Breaking down into a tearless sob, I prayed, pleading for help. I wasn't sweating anymore. *Bad sign*. I prayed for health and strength. I prayed I'd have no run-ins with snakes and shuddered at the mere thought. I prayed for peace and wisdom. I prayed to overcome this trial. I prayed for a miracle.

Chapter 6

It was late afternoon. The sun's rays stretched far across the denim blue sky, blinding me with their brilliance. Hours had passed and terror set in with a vengeance. Maybe I *should* have listened to my mom about wearing an emergency whistle around my neck. I shrugged and murmured to myself, "No one would be around to hear it anyways. That's the blessing and curse of being so far out in nature."

I hadn't seen or heard Chase in awhile. I anxiously called out his name … no sign of him. I sent up a prayer asking that he be kept safe, wherever he was. I wished hadn't wolfed down all the snacks in my pocket during the hike. Even having a single Jolly Rancher left would have been helpful. A glorious and wonderful watermelon Jolly Rancher.

I let out a long sigh. My morale was slipping. Hopelessness had burrowed its home in my heart. Shading my eyes from the sun, I gazed out across the vast landscape, completely void of human life. "Think Callie, think," I commanded myself. "What would grandpa's advice be?"

With a half-smile I almost heard him say, "Callie, you

listen up and you listen real good. Take some deep breaths. Quiet your mind. Pray . . . Then get to work. The Lord helps those who help themselves."

"But grandpa," I talked as if he were there, "I've tried though. I've *really* tried and I don't see how I can get out of here with my hurt ankle. And even if I could get out, it's *miles* back to my Jeep. I don't want to give up. I am no quitter, you know that. But I just don't know what I can do."

When I didn't hear a response, I jolted to the present with the realization that he wasn't there. I was hallucinating. This was all in my head.

My stomach sank further as I realized no one knew I was here. A perk of my job is that there's a lot of field work. The rest of my work can be done anywhere with my laptop and an internet connection, usually my couch with Chase by my side. My boss knew I'd be checking on three different sites this week, but he didn't know which site I'd be at on which day. No one would be expecting me back. This was an unexpected downer about my practically non-existent dating life. *And*, I hadn't told my parents because I didn't want *yet another* lecture about the dangers of hiking by myself.

After I finished my millionth prayer, I looked around the bare ledge, hoping somehow *this* time I'd see something, *anything*, I had missed before that could help. I tried to scan with fresh eyes. I tried to think with an open mind. *What would MacGyver do?* My brain tensed as I willed out of the box ideas to appear. *Nothing.*

I sprung up straighter when I heard a bark in the

distance. My spirits lifted as I strained to hear. I hoped Chase would make his way back to me, I hadn't seen him for hours. I was worried about him . . . and lonely.

There it was again! A faint bark came from farther up the canyon. I didn't want to get my hopes up, but it sounded so real I couldn't help but be optimistic. Then as suddenly as the sound had come, all was silent.

Another hallucination. My heart sank to the black hole in my stomach.

An eternity had passed and still nothing. Time turned slowly, yet the sun rapidly dipped towards the horizon. I was nervous about the approaching night. It was a new moon tonight and my flashlight was in the backpack. In a couple hours it was going to get pitch black. While contemplating how I'd handle the long dark night I was abruptly interrupted by the faint duet of a horse whinny and a dog barking. The noise was coming closer!

And then I heard it, a man's glorious voice saying, "Okay, okay, I hear ya girl." Followed by an offended bark.

"Uh oh," I silently giggled to myself.

Then I heard him chuckle, "Oh pardon me, *sir*!"

After the initial shock of realizing I may actually be saved, I felt foolish as it dawned on me that I wouldn't be saved if he didn't know I was there. He might think Chase is a stray. I can't be this close to being rescued and just sit here stupefied.

"Help! Help! Down here!" my raspy voice called out in barely more than a whisper. "Oh please help me," I whimpered. Realizing he wouldn't be able to hear my pitiful pleas, I grabbed two loose rocks and started banging them together with all the strength my aching arms could muster.

Chase's barks got closer. I scooted to the ledge, straining to see. Chase was running towards me, and thank the heavens above, a man leading a dark bay horse was following! *A beautiful mirage.* An angel looking like a young John Wayne here to whisk me off into a wondrous dream.

I hoarsely called out again for help after realizing that this gorgeous guy wasn't a hallucination but was indeed *very* real.

I watched as "Mr. Picturesque Epitome of the Perfect Man" looked for the source of the sound, then saw me. Alarmed, he sprinted to me. Leaning over the ledge, he anxiously asked, "Are you okay? How long have you been down there? How badly are you hurt?"

Dazed, I stared up at him, admiring his physique. His chambray shirt rolled to his elbows was amazingly flattering on him. "Can you stand up on your own?" he asked, startling me out of my dreamy state. "If you can reach up to me, I will pull you up."

I nodded and cautiously stood. He laid on his stomach and reached over the boulders' edge. "Okay, I'm ready. Give me your hands." Stretching my arms towards him, I raised on to my left tippy toes, while keeping my right knee bent. My balance was wobbly, but before I tipped over our fingers touched. Electricity shot through my veins. He firmly grabbed me and began pulling me up.

My eyes locked onto the bulging muscles of his

tanned forearms. *Wow he's strong.* As I got higher, he scooted backwards. With a final strong tug he fell back, pulling me with him. As I awkwardly toppled onto his lap, he laughed, "Whoa, easy there."

I sat in his lap longer than was necessary because I was too tired to move and . . . I didn't want to let him go. Gazing up at his gorgeous face, his worried blue eyes fixated on me, I deliriously blurted out, "I think I love you!"

He smiled at me, amusement evident on his face. "What's your name?"

"Callie," I replied while gawking at him.

"I'm Alexander. It's nice to meet you."

I giggled feverishly while feeling mortified at my schoolgirl stupidity.

He carefully set me on the ground beside him and said, "Callie I'm going to get you some water, and then I need to look over your injuries. Is that alright with you?"

I tilted my head slightly, trying to memorize his wildly attractive face, then nodded in agreement.

He handed me his canteen, then placed his hands over mine when he noticed me trembling to hold it steady as I drank. It was hard to swallow, but after that first sip the cool water eased the pain in my throat.

He felt my forehead and promptly poured water in his hand and splashed it on my face and neck. Water had never felt so wonderful. Alexander carried me to the shade and ripped off pieces off the bottom of his shirt to bandage my worst cuts and scrapes. I was conscious of Chase carefully watching me, I smiled gratefully at him and told him what a good boy he was. Alexander yanked a blue bandana out from his pocket, drenched it with water, then loosely tied it around my neck.

He examined my ankle next and said he thought it was a sprain and not broken. "I'm sorry," he said, "this is probably going to hurt, but I need to get the boot off your foot. I'm concerned about the swelling." He looked at me enquiringly. "Squeeze onto my arm if you need to." I nodded and he began to gently loosen my laces. A yelp escaped my lips when he tugged the boot. "I'm so sorry," he murmured. Once it was off though, I felt immediate relief.

After assessing the situation, we determined the best course of action was to take me to his ranch. It'd be a shorter distance than to hike to my car and drive back to town. And there was *no way* I could've managed the hike out, or operate a vehicle.

I would normally be worried about going to a strange man's house, but for some reason I felt comfortable and safe with Alexander . . . And I was tired, *so dang tired.* I was ready to lean on somebody who seemed so capable and strong . . . and gorgeous. Being a single woman can be exhausting and sometimes we just need a hero. A handsome man to swoop in and save the day.

Chapter 7

Alexander helped me onto his horse, and I sank comfortably into the leather saddle. He gathered my belongings, tied my hiking boot by its laces to the backpack, then slung it over his shoulders. He guided us back to his ranch while Chase happily ran alongside him.

A steady climb brought us deeper into the canyon, up a steep switchback trail, and over a hillside thick with pinyon pines and patches of scrub oak with vibrant red leaves.

As we journeyed on Alexander casually asked me what brought me here, about my work, and my life. Exhaustion caused my responses to be basic and vague.

We stopped to give the animals a minute to rest before starting the descent down the other side. He encouraged me to drink what water was left from his canteen. I thanked him again, for *everything*. He smiled sweetly at me and said, "My pleasure," as he took the reins and began walking down the gentle slope.

I watched him from the saddle, relishing the fact that I could gaze adoringly at him unnoticed. He walked with an unpretentious swagger. He didn't realize how attractive he was and I decided I was more than okay with his humility; cockiness is a turn off anyways.

Every so often Alexander would glance over his shoulder at me, his eyebrow cocked and his eyes dazzling with curiosity and concern. I'd avert my gaze and pretend I was interested in the passing trees, an interesting rock, a lone cloud floating slowly across the sky . . . *anything*. Then I'd casually look to him like I hadn't been intensely staring at him seconds earlier. We'd smile, he'd ask how I was, I'd say, "I'm fine, really." Then he'd give a satisfied nod and turn back to the trail ahead.

After awhile, the steady rhythm of the horse's gait and the cool evening air, combined for a moment of repose. Alexander must've glanced back at me as I started to doze off in the saddle. He stopped leading the horse and hopped up behind me. He held me in his strong arms, letting my bobbing head rest back on his shoulder.

He started to sing tenderly, lulling me further. I felt safe and secure, like a little kid tucked into bed with extra blankets on a snowy winter's night. My eyes got heavier with every clop of the horse's hooves. I heard Alexander's low voice softly sing "You're the Nearest Thing to Heaven" by Johnny Cash.

After I had awakened, he murmured in my ear, "So how exactly did you happen to fall?" I told him in detail about seeing the white doe. He was captivated and amazed.

He told me his grandfather used to tell him a story

about seeing a white doe. "But I always thought it was just a tall tale, grandpa trying to pull my leg. My grandpa said there was something magical about the canyons in this area, and that every fifty or so years a white doe sighting would happen. A spirit animal presenting itself to those worthy or in need."

"My grandpa saw one too!" I interjected.

"Really? That's incredible! Though I will say I am feeling pretty left out." He laughed, then squeezed me tighter and said, "Keep your eyes open for this upcoming view."

The sun was setting as we crested a low hill, golden light cast a pastel glow on a ranch nestled in the valley below. There was a picturesque meadow filled with grazing cattle and a creek that wound through it. Near a two-story stone and log house was an intricately laid out orchard and several outbuildings interspersed on the property.

"Welcome to Cadence Creek Ranch, been in my family for generations."

"Wow, it's beautiful. Absolutely *stunning* actually."

Alexander then proceeded to tell me how his great-grandfather settled this valley. He spent summers and any weekend he could with his grandparents. His dad was an only child and didn't want the ranch, so it went to Alexander when his grandparents passed.

"This has always been *home* for me, my soul belongs here," he said with a tone of reverence.

"I can certainly see why. There's a hallowed feeling here," I replied and wiped a stray tear. "I'm in awe."

As we meandered through the meadow and rode passed cows chewing their dinner, Alexander said, "I've got a joke for ya, courtesy of my grandpa. What do you get from a pampered cow? Spoiled milk."

I laughed, "Oh so your grandpa told corny jokes too?"

"Yeah I think it's required that once you reach a certain age you *have* to tell 'dad jokes' or else . . . I don't know what . . . you'll get banned from eating Costco samples for your lunch . . . *for life*."

"Now *that* would be a cruel punishment," I said while laughing harder.

An Australian Shepherd dog that waited on the front porch came running to us. Hopping off the horse Alexander called out, "Hey Peaches! How are ya girl?" She wagged her tail happily while he scratched behind her ears and said, "Peaches, this is Chase, and that pretty lady there is Callie." As if on cue, Peaches ran over to Chase, they sniffed each other eagerly as dogs do, and ran off together towards the house. Fast friends. I was relieved they were getting along so well.

"She's adorable!" I gushed.

"Peaches would rather hang out on the porch than go for long trips. She enjoys naps and food," he said.

Chapter 8

The sun had set as we reached his house. The transcendent painting in the sky had faded into night and silver stars dotted the midnight blue sky. Alexander carried me inside, cradled in his arms. I heard him mumble to himself that he'd always wanted to carry a woman across his threshold like in the old movies. I tried to pretend I hadn't heard what he said, but couldn't stop the pleased smile tugging at the corners of my mouth.

Walking through the entryway, Alexander paused to toss his hat onto a cast iron stand. This was the first time I got a good look at his hair. He had a full head of magnificent wavy brown hair that just *begged* to be touched. I resisted the urge to run my fingers through it. His boots clanking on the wood floor brought my attention back. He carefully sat me on his worn leather couch, saying, "I'll be back in a couple minutes, just need to take care of my horse. No need to worry, be back in a jiffy."

"Okay," I said as I smiled up at him, his eyes twinkled back at mine.

I sank deeper into the comfortable cushions and decided to never leave. After sitting for hours, first, on my butt, out in nature, and then in a saddle, a couch was now my favorite thing ever. I was *exhausted*, more tired than ever before in my life. Thankfully I hadn't sustained any injuries that needed immediate medical attention. Plenty of rest was what my body needed most.

I looked around, taking in the juxtaposition of rustic cabin meets modern ranch house. A masculine home, but cozy and inviting. Three walls of the living room were made from big logs and to my right was a massive rock fireplace. The masonry work was exceptional. On the walls hung a few cowboy paintings, landscape photography of the Southwest, and an old acoustic guitar.

"What do ya think?" Alexander asked with a tentative smile and curious eyes. Startled, I whipped my head around and saw him leaning against the doorway to the kitchen. He must've come in through the back door. The site of him startled me again. *Dang* he was good looking.

"It's charming," I replied slightly breathless.

I glanced at the bag in his left hand as he walked into the room and said, "I have some presents for you." And immediately gave me a bottle of ibuprofen. He stole pillows from the other sofa to elevate my leg with and placed a bag of frozen corn wrapped in a dish towel on my ankle. He rushed back into the kitchen and returned with a big glass of ice water.

He felt my head with the back of his hand, pursed his lips and turned back into his kitchen to grab a damp cloth. He gently caressed my forehead with it. It was cool and refreshing. He cleaned and bandaged my cuts and scrapes, turned on the ceiling fan, and I peacefully dozed off.

I awoke later to a reverberating rumble and looked around, confused. My eyes flickered to the fireplace where Alexander sat in a rocking chair watching me intently. Embarrassed, I jolted up as my stomach growled again. *Perfect timing.* "You're like a grizzly bear straight out of hibernation." He laughed, then more seriously said, "I'm relieved your temperature finally came down. I lit a fire because this high desert country cools off a lot at night and you started to shiver." He nodded towards me and I noticed a crocheted afghan covering me. He must've placed it there while I slept . . . *how sweet.*

I thanked him but frowned after noticing Chase and Peaches both lounging at his feet. I was jealous Chase had given his allegiance away so fast, and I said so. Alexander told me he had cooked Chase a big steak as a reward for being so heroic. I laughed and conceded it *was* well deserved. Scratching Chase behind the ears he said, "You're a good boy. You're like a real-life Shadow from Homeward Bound."

"Well usually he's more like Chance," I giggled.

I thanked Alexander for being so kind and for looking after Chase and myself. Wary of being a burden, I told him if he would drive me to my Jeep, I could make it home alright.

"It's pretty late. You are welcome to stay here tonight." He looked worried about being presumptuous and quickly added, "Or I can drive you home, if you want.

No offense, but you're in no condition to drive yourself."

Alexander assured me again that he is a gentleman and honorable. "I know. I sense that about you." Then glanced down and whispered, "You're my hero."

I agreed it was probably best to stay the night, but mostly because I didn't want to say goodbye to him yet! He insisted on at least calling someone for me to let them know I was alright. "There's no cell service here but we do have an old school landline," he said.

I *should* let someone know where I was, staying alone in a strange man's house and all, but also did *not* want to explain to my parents, or anyone else, the circumstances leading to this situation. He chuckled at my independent stubbornness.

We looked at each other in wonder and softly talked about everything and nothing.

Another growl of my stomach and we both laughed. I also started to feel an urgent need for a bathroom break . . . I guess I did guzzle a lot of water earlier. Breaking the spell of his intense gaze he offered, "Here, let me help you." He put a muscular arm around me and helped me up.

On the way to the bathroom he mentioned he might have crutches out in a shed that he'd look for later. I secretly wished to use *him* as a crutch . . . *forever*.

Appalled by my appearance in the bathroom mirror, I hurried to freshen up as best as I could. Butterflies took flight in my stomach as I put on Alexander's basketball shorts and rodeo t-shirt that he grabbed for me to wear. They smelt like him, absolutely divine!

When Alexander noticed me hobbling down the

hallway, he sped over and swooped me up in his arms. *A girl could get used to this*. He brought me into the kitchen and sat me onto a bar stool. He handed me a big glass of water saying, "Drink up sweetheart and I'll whip us up a late meal. Any preferences?"

I giggled, "Nope." Then stammered, "I mean *yes,* I'll drink the water, but *nope* I don't have any preferences . . . for food, that is."

With a smoldering smile he said, "Quesadillas it is then." He winked and turned to open the vintage refrigerator. A blush burned my cheeks, so I tried to nonchalantly look around. Behind me was a large farmhouse table, it looked well loved. I smiled at the thought of so many past family meals eaten there. With a navy blue wall behind it, and big windows to its right, it looked like such a peaceful place to gather.

I watched Alexander as he cooked on a huge old-fashioned cast iron stove. He caught my eye and we both smiled. I tried to play it cool and continued my casual browsing. I admired his kitchen; the live edge pine cabinets, walnut countertops, and an antique white enameled cast iron sink that looked to be original to the house.

"Your kitchen is amazing! Your whole house is," I commented.

Turning to me with a humble smile he said, "Thank you. The log portion of the house was part of the original two room cabin, built by my great-grandpa. Then in the late 1950's my grandpa renovated and added on a couple rooms and a second story. Since then it hadn't changed much, so when I inherited this place it needed extensive repairs."

"Wow, I can imagine. It's cool this has been in your family for so long! You can feel the rich family history in these walls."

"If only they could talk, huh?" he chuckled.

"Totally! That's an awesome chandelier," I said, pointing to the chandelier above the dining table. It was made from horseshoes welded together in an intricate design with candelabra lightbulbs.

"Thanks, my great-grandpa made that. When I renovated, I found it in the barn, all it needed was a little cleaning and to be rewired. I actually pulled a few of these relics out of the barn," he said gesturing to all the antiques. "My parents think I'm crazy, but I like it." He shrugged.

"Well I think your parents are crazy for thinking you're crazy," I said smiling. "It's thrifty to rescue these treasures. Plus, from a decorating standpoint, it's eclectic and makes your home completely artistic and unique. I love it!"

"Well thank you," he blushed. "I'm glad you like it. Dinners ready," he said sliding a teal plate in front of me with one perfectly golden quesadilla.

After we ate in companionable silence Alexander helped me back to the couch. He put an old western movie in the DVD player and dimmed the lights. My heart raced as he grabbed a blanket and sat right next to me instead of in the rocking chair. He put a pillow on his lap and swung my right leg gently over to it.

It felt natural to sit together intimately like this. Snuggled under a blanket with the dogs snoring by the fire. We started the movie, but I was distracted by the way the fire glowed on Alexander's handsome face. The light enhanced his glistening blue eyes and the shadows deepened the stubble along his jaw. I continued to stealthily gaze at him until exhaustion caught up with me. As my breathing began to slow the song "Forever in Blue Jeans" fluttered through my mind.

Snuggled into the well-worn couch, covered with a patchwork quilt and crocheted afghan; I had the irreplaceable warm feeling that comes when a kind heart is beating close by. I drifted off into a deep and restful sleep. Dreaming of heroes on horses, cowboys and knights, old western movie stars . . . all with the handsome face of my rescuer, Alexander.

Chapter 9

A radiant light filtered through the windowpanes as I slowly woke up. Feeling well rested, I tried to roll over but groaned from the soreness shooting through my body.

My eyes instantly alert, I tried to take in the unfamiliar surroundings. I was confused, then with a flash, the pain coming from my throbbing ankle triggered my memory.

With fresh eyes and morning light I noticed details I hadn't seen last night. There was a Navajo rug beneath the log coffee table and on one wall old photographs artfully hung in mismatched picture frames.

As I looked around I noticed a tray on the coffee table. Sitting up to look closer, I smiled at the site of a little bouquet of purple and white wildflowers in a mason jar and a big plate of breakfast . . . complete with a glass of orange juice.

Next to it was the bottle of ibuprofen and a note with my name on it.

Curious, I snatched the paper and my insides fluttered as I began to read.

Callie,

I've gone out to do the morning chores. Both dogs are with me, so don't worry about Chase. 1 hope you slept well. Take some ibuprofen after you eat breakfast. 1 washed your pants, but your shirt is bloody and tattered beyond repair, so you can borrow my shirt that's on the coffee table. 1 put a barstool in the shower for you. Help yourself to whatever you need. Sorry 1 could only find one crutch. See you soon.

-Alexander

After eating the delicious breakfast, I stood and grabbed the old crutch leaning against the coffee table. Picking up the stack of clothes I sighed just imagining how gorgeous Alexander must look in the dark blue flannel shirt.

On the way to the bathroom I paused to look at the county fair blue ribbons pinned on the wall. With a slight nod of approval I said to myself, "Biggest pumpkin? Impressive."

Sitting on the barstool in the shower I looked around at the beautiful river rocks mortared on the walls and floor. As the rainfall showerhead drizzled down on me, I reached for the 2-in-1 shampoo and laughed, "Man stuff."

I wished for a long soak in the clawfoot tub opposite the shower but knew I wouldn't be able to get in and out of it unassisted. And *no way* was I going to ask for assistance. I'm not that kind of girl. Regardless, the nearly scalding water and steam from the shower felt heavenly on my sore muscles.

After dressing, I used the new toothbrush Alexander

had thoughtfully set on the counter for me, along with a container of pine gum salve and other toiletries. I carefully braided my tangled wet hair and put on lip balm.

Wishing I carried makeup and a brush in my backpack, I resolutely decided to start being extra prepared in the future and start following the Boy Scout motto, "Be Prepared." Not sure they meant carrying mascara and lip gloss as being prepared, but girl rules are different . . . and necessities *are* necessities. Wanting to look pretty for an incredibly handsome man is *not* a crime.

I made my way down the hallway feeling infinitely better now that I was free from all that crusty blood, sweat, and tears. Alexander was waiting for me in the front room and I suddenly felt dizzy from the site of him. I leaned more on the crutch, thankful for its stability.

"How are ya feelin'?" he asked as he raked a hand through his dark hair, glancing at me with a shy smile.

"I'm good, thanks. And thanks for everything this morning, that was really sweet of you," I replied, my brown eyes twinkling at him in return.

"Yep. Glad to hear it," he said as his gaze moved down my body to my feet. I would've assumed he was just checking on my ankle if it wasn't for the look of longing in his eyes and a breathless "wow" that escaped his lips. Flattered, I bit my lip, but was embarrassed by the blush burning my face. The bright red of it was probably visible despite my sunburnt cheeks.

"You ready to head into town? Have old Doc check you out?" He coughed and quickly said, "Your ankle, I mean. Have old Doc check out your *ankle*."

I laughed. "Yeah I'm ready, but you really don't have to go through all this trouble. If you could just drive me over to get my Jeep, I can drive myself—"

He put a hand up. "Nonsense. It's no trouble at all. And don't worry about Chase. He and Peaches are out *helping* the ranch hands. They'll be fine while we're gone."

♦ ✳ ♦

I hobbled outside with the one crutch, feeling like Tiny Tim. Seeing Alexander's ranch in the morning light took my breath away, it was *stunning*. Dewy pastures sparkled in the sun and orchard leaves tinged with gold danced in the morning breeze. The air was crisp and full of life. At this moment I felt a new chapter begin.

Alexander held open the door to his old, robin's egg blue truck for me. After he helped me inside he flung the crutch into the truck bed. He pulled me over to sit in the middle next to him and told me to prop my right leg up on the seat. The woven cotton fabric had a cool vintage pattern and was comfortably cushioned. *They don't make trucks like they used to.*

We drove along a well-maintained dirt road through spectacular Southwestern scenery. As we drove over a

narrow, wood plank bridge I asked, "Cadence Creek?"
Nodding out the window to the small creek lined with
cottonwood trees.

"Yep, that's it."

"It's pretty."

"Yep, it sure is."

I tried to suppress my smirk at his "man of few words"
persona. After awhile Alexander put his arm around me,
and I leaned against him with a sigh of contentment. He
smelled *so* good.

Eventually the road came to a highway which we
turned left onto and continued towards town. As we drove
the song "Dying Breed" by The Killers played on the
radio. I smiled at the lyrics, feeling like they were
depicting who Alexander and I were becoming.

As we arrived at the doctor's office, the receptionist
smiled fondly at Alexander. Immediate concern took over
her features when she noticed me. *Yeah I know I look bad
lady.*

"Hi Florence. Is Doc in?" Alexander asked.

Standing up she answered, "Yes, luckily you caught
him right before his lunch break. Follow me please."

We walked into a small exam room and an older man
immediately greeted us. His bushy white eyebrows lifted.
"Well hello miss." Then noting the crutch he joked,
"What'd Alexander here do to ya? Stomp on ya dancing

with those two left feet of his?"

"Whoa!" Alexander put his arms up, feigning offence, then wagged his finger at the doctor, "I'll have you know I'm actually a pretty decent dancer."

The doctor chuckled, while my curiosity piqued. Butterflies fluttered at the thought of dancing with Alexander.

After a thorough exam, he concluded that my ankle was sprained and *not* broken, *thank goodness*. As we stood to leave the doctor handed us each a sucker with a dramatic flourish and a wink.

Chapter 10

Walking, or rather *hobbling* along the cracked sidewalk to his truck, Alexander asked me with a hopeful smile, "How about some lunch? My treat."

"Yes to lunch, but I couldn't let you pay," I protested. "You've already done more than enough to help me. I need to repay you for your kindness. Let me pay for lunch at least!"

With sincerity in his eyes he insisted, "Callie, it has been my pleasure, really. And no way are you paying. I'm a gentleman, it'd hurt my street cred or something if you paid."

"Oh your street cred huh?" I giggled. "Well okay, if you're sure?" I asked timidly then added, "I really would like to somehow show my thanks to you though."

"Being my date to lunch is more than enough," he said as he opened the truck door for me.

As we drove a few blocks through town toward main street, Alexander took it upon himself to be my tour guide. Pointing out landmarks, he said in an official voice, "To your left there is the United States Postal Service, where you get your mail." I giggled and he continued the tour,

"This is an old church, built sometime in the 1800's. It's now home to our town's museum. And here is where I went to high school . . . and where both of my parents happen to work."

"Wait, did your parents work there while you were in school?"

"Yep. Having both parents work at the high school made my school experience *extra* fun, note my sarcasm. My dad's the math teacher, and my mom's a secretary. They were chaperones at my homecoming, prom . . ." He rolled his eyes. "Everything."

I groaned with pity. "Sounds rough."

"You have no idea," he said and we both burst into laughter. Then he continued, "My mom especially loved using the intercom. She thought of it as her own personal communication device. One time the Principal had to ban her from using it. For two months the other secretary was the only one allowed to make announcements."

"Really? Why?" I asked.

Alexander looked away from me and to the road. His face heated with a crimson blush. He cleared his throat and admitted, "Well, one time during my sophomore year, I worked as a teacher's aid for my dad. It was during fourth period. It was the one period in the day that he didn't have a class. Since it was usually just he and I in his classroom during that time, my mom would often communicate to us through the intercom. She reminded us about appointments, nagged my dad for not taking out the trash the night before, stuff like that. But this one time . . . she mistakenly broadcast her message to the entire school."

"Uh-oh." I grimaced.

Alexander lowered his head in shame and slowly shook it side to side. "I can't believe I'm about to tell you this. I had an upset stomach that doomed day my mom's voice said over the loudspeaker, 'Alexander sweetie, don't forget to stop by the office during your lunch break for another dose of Pepto-Bismol . . . Oh and sweetie, I brought an extra pair of undies for you, just in case you get smears.'"

I gasped. "No!"

"Yep. I could hear her infernal voice echoing through the hallways, followed by the roar of laughter from my peers emanating from every single classroom. I can still hear their hysterics ringing in my mind."

"I am so sorry! That's so embarrassing! What did you do?" I asked.

"Well, my dad took me home and I refused to go back to school for a week. When I did return, the senior class had two new nicknames for me, 'Pepto' and 'Skidmark Sweetie' . . . which they called me for the rest of the year by the way . . . it was bad."

"That's awful!"

"Yeah, I can find the humor in it now though," he said as his frown turned into a smirk and a low chuckle escaped his lips. His laugh was contagious and soon I was howling. I bent over to grab my sides, panting for breath.

"I'm sorry to laugh!" I managed to choke out, "It's so awful it's hilarious!"

Alexander grinned at me as I wiped stray tears from my face. Clearing his throat in a mock authoritarian way he continued, "Excuse me miss, back to the tour. The town park is to your left." He pointed out the window. "That place there, with the big grass field, and the playground." He teased, "Can't miss it."

"Thanks," I said, feigning gratitude, then laughed, "I don't know how I ever would have recognized it, if not for your obvious description."

He smiled. "And here's the fine establishment we'll be dining at today, The Burger Barn Café." I grinned at him, amusement and attraction twinkling in both our eyes. "Would you like to eat inside, or at the park?"

"Ohhh, definitely the park. I love picnics. Why is it that food *always* tastes better when eaten outside?"

"Science," he stated matter-of-factly, then we both erupted into giggling again.

I sat at a booth near the entrance while Alexander stood at the counter ordering our food. The song "Electric Love" filled the café with its upbeat music while I admired the view. Alexander looked *amazing* in those jeans.

With the goods procured we walked outside. Alexander stopped by his truck, handed me an Oreo milkshake, and grabbed a blanket tucked behind the seat. We took our lunch across the street to the town park.

"We better eat the Oreo shake first, you know, so it doesn't melt." He smiled innocently. "I'm just trying to do the responsible thing here."

"I see the wisdom in that," I readily agreed.

Alexander swiftly spread the blanket onto the cool grass, dropped the greasy bags onto it, then helped me sit. He pulled two plastic red spoons from his back pocket, handed one to me, and we went to work. *Perfection.*

Next was a BLT for me, and a burger for him. As we flirted between bites, my heart glowed with love and contentment. Before meeting Alexander, I never believed people could fall in love so fast. I had been struck by Cupid and hoped Alexander felt the same way.

"Oh, I almost forgot!" he said as he wiped his fingers on a napkin and pulled a necklace out of his pocket. "Here, I got this for you in the café." He handed me a lovely handmade necklace with a deer design etched onto a wood pendant.

"It's perfect!" I gushed. "Thank you so much! Help me put it on."

Goosebumps emerged on the back of my neck as he moved my braided hair to the side and brushed his fingers lightly across my skin. His big hands fumbled with the clasp. Once secured, he looked at me and I felt the voltage of love igniting between us. The union of our souls was palpable. I coyly smiled into his smoldering eyes.

The spell was disrupted as three kids raced passed us towards the playground, squealing the whole way. Alexander crumpled up our wrappers, tossed them in an empty bag, and grabbed the bag loaded with fries. We continued to chat as we polished them off.

Alexander smirked at me, "You've got some ketchup on your face." I cringed. *Typical.* As I reached for the stack of napkins, he beat me to them, saying, "Here, allow me."

He leaned over and dabbed at the left corner of my mouth and chin. I looked away thoroughly embarrassed. I glanced at him when he dropped the napkin, but his hand hadn't left my face.

Our eyes locked and he caressed my face. He gradually leaned in, wrapped his other hand around to the small of my back, supporting me, as he slowly came in for a kiss.

Alexander's lips skillfully pressed against mine. My arms automatically draped around his neck, and my fingers wove into his wavy hair. As his lips lingered on mine, electricity sparked through my veins. Fireworks burst all around me, lighting up my life with his love.

He broke the seal of our lips to whisper, "Callie, I'm in love with you."

Alexander held me passionately as our lips intertwined and our kiss intensified. My senses swirled with delight.

I was entirely enchanted by him.

As we kissed, the sun's rays beamed down on us. I knew with all my heart that my grandpa was right. Seeing a white doe *changes* you. They truly *did* bring good fortune. And what greater fortune to receive than to find your soulmate. To discover for yourself the kind of love written in the stars.

Alexander's stubble brushed against my face as I clung to him, feeling the muscles in his arm tighten around me in return. I felt his strength, but more importantly, I could feel the strength of his character . . . and I knew my heart had finally found its home.

Rock Art *Romance*

Playlist

"Return of the Grievous Angel"
Gram Parsons

"Take Me Home, Country Roads"
John Denver

"Hello Sunshine"
Bruce Springsteen

"Song in Stone"
Iron & Wine

"Stay Alive"
José González

"I Think I Love You"
The Partridge Family

"Caution"
The Killers

"You're the Nearest Thing to Heaven"
Johnny Cash

"Maybe I'm Amazed"
Paul McCartney

"Forever in Blue Jeans"
Neil Diamond

"Dying Breed"
The Killers

"Electric Love"
Børns